Beasty

Bath

by ROBERT NEUBECKER

ORCHARD BOOKS ● NEW YORK

AN IMPRINT OF SCHOLASTIC INC.

Library of Congress Cataloging-in-Publication Data
Neubecker, Robert. Beasty Bath / written and illustrated by Robert Neubecker. 1st. ed. p. cm.
Summary: A young child's imagination transforms bath time into a monster-filled adventure.
ISBN: 0-439-64000-8
[1. Imagination—Fiction. 2. Monsters—Fiction. 3. Baths—Fiction. 4. Stories in Rhyme.] I. Title.
PZ8.3.N3676 Be 2005   [E] 22

10 9 8 7 6 5 4 3 2   05 06 07 08 09

Printed in Singapore   46
Reinforced Binding for Library Use
First edition, October 2005

The art was created using watercolor and ink.
The text was set in 32-point Locarno Light.
The display was set in CircusDog.
Book design by Marijka Kostiw

For Ruth,
Iz, & Jo

SPECIAL THANKS

TO KARA BANG & TAYLOR GOODNOE

The evening's come, I hear a roar,

it's time to catch my dinosaur.

Into the bath with bubbles so high,

I will carry you—away we fly!

Sailing on a soapy blue sea,

scrubbing your feet, all thirty-three.

Clean your claws, your fur and scales,

now wash your beasty horns and tails.

Shampoo your beasty mane of glory,

soon we will read a bedtime story!

Shine up each horn and polish each feature,

here is my sparkly little creature!

Dry off your coat and stand up tall,

you are the cleanest beast of all.

Clean your fangs, now do not rush,

be careful not to eat the brush!

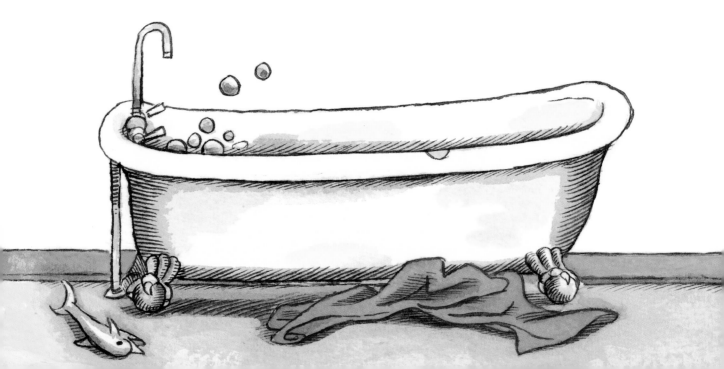

To bed you go, warm, snug, and tight,

your friends will be with you all

through the night.

Put out the light, it is time to sleep,

to rest and dream in the forest deep.

The jungle is quiet, all is at peace,

good night, sleep tight, my sweet

little beast.